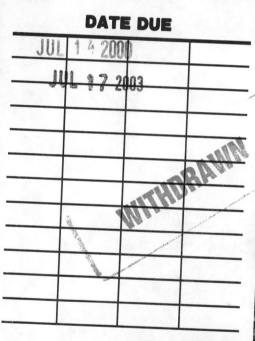

DATE DUE

JUL 1 4 2000	
JUL 1 7 2003	

WITHDRAWN

Demco No. 62-0549

CLOSE

CLOSER

CLOSEST

Shelley Rotner and Richard Olivo

Atheneum Books for Young Readers

Atheneum Books for Young Readers
An imprint of Simon & Schuster
Children's Publishing Division
1230 Avenue of the Americas
New York, New York 10020

Book design by Michael Nelson
The text of this book is set in Helvetica.

Printed in Hong Kong
First Edition
10 9 8 7 6 5 4 3 2

Library of Congress Cataloging-in-Publication Data
Rotner, Shelley.
Close, closer, closest / Shelley Rotner, Richard Olivo.—1st ed.
p.   cm.
Summary: Introduces perspective and scale through
pictures of objects taken from three different distances.
ISBN 0-689-80762-7
1. Size perception—Juvenile literature. [1. Size perception.]
I. Olivo, Richard II. Title.
BF299.S5R67   1997
152.14'2—dc20
96-15837

For Camille, Emily, Felix, Gretchen, Nicholas, Sarah, and Taryn
—S. R. and R. O.

Leaves on a tree . . .

See the pattern
on a leaf.

A butterfly . . .

has rows

of scales

on its wing.

A sunflower . . .

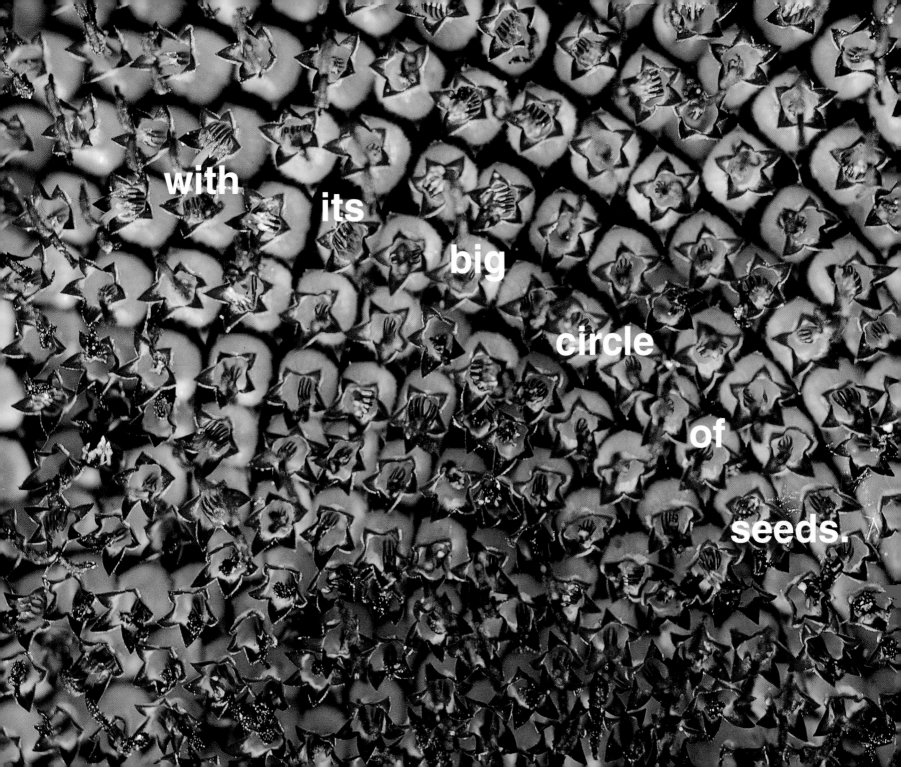

with its big circle of seeds.

A cookie . . .

with
round
rainbow
sprinkles.

A bowl of cereal . . .

with
bubbles
in the
milk.

Strawberries!

They have

many

little seeds.

The pictures in a comic book . . .

are

made

of tiny

colored

dots.

A peacock's feather . . .

is

made

of

lines

of

brilliant

color.

A dog . . .

with
multicolored
hair.

Paint . . .

on
the
bristles
of
a
brush.

A glove . . .

knitted

of colored

yarn.

A
handful
of
coins . . .

the face on a dime.

**An image on a
TV screen . . .**

is made of red, green, and blue stripes.

Take a good look . . .

up close!

How Big is Big? (For kids and parents)

Most of the pictures in this book were made with an ordinary camera. The closest pictures, however, were either photographed through a microscope or taken with a special lens that makes the objects appear larger and closer than you could normally see them with the naked eye. You can create a similar effect by looking through a magnifying glass. Do you notice anything new about the objects that you didn't notice before?

How can we tell how **big** an object really is? One way is to photograph a second object whose size is known, like the ruler in this picture. This acts as a scale and lets us know the real size of the first object, no matter how big or small we make the final picture. In this photograph, the ruler tells us that the magnified section of a penny is 9 millimeters tall, or about a third of an inch.

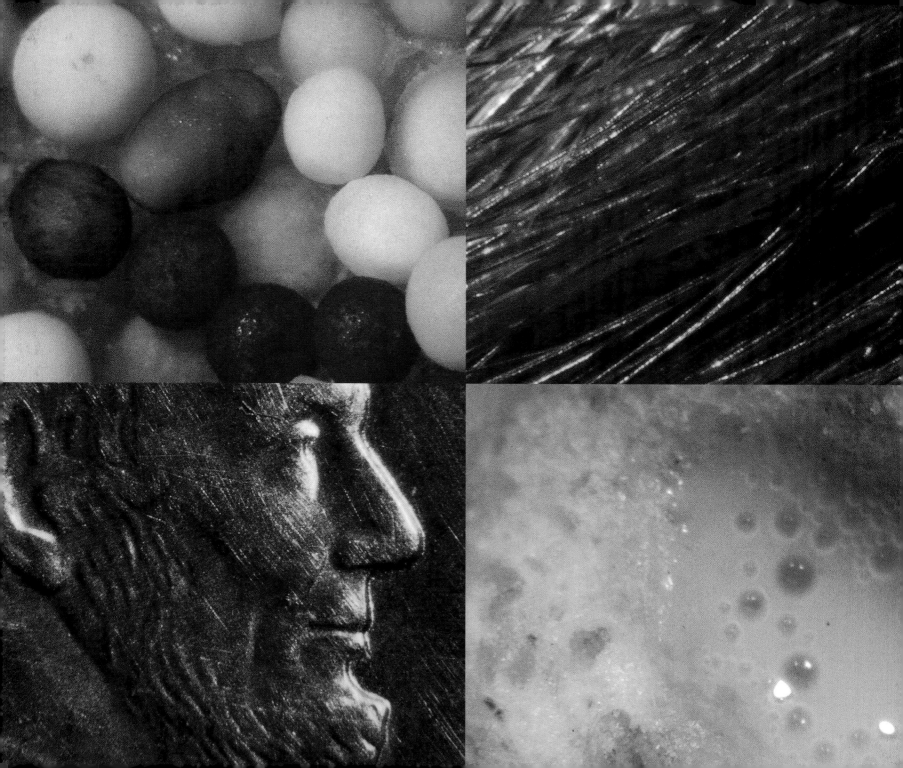